SASHA AND THE WOLF-CHILD

Collins
RED
Storybook

Sasha
and the
Wolf-Child

Ann Jungman

Illustrated by Giles Greenfield

Collins
An imprint of HarperCollinsPublishers

First published in Great Britain by
CollinsChildren'sBooks 1999

3 5 7 9 8 6 4 2

CollinsChildren'sBooks is a division of
HarperCollins*Publishers* Ltd, 77-85 Fulham Palace Road,
Hammersmith, London W6 8JB

The HarperCollins website address is
www.**fire**and**water**.com

Text copyright © Ann Jungman 1999
Illustrations copyright © Giles Greenfield 1999

The author and illustrator assert the moral right to
be identified as the author and illustrator of the work.

Printed and bound in Great Britain by
Omnia Books Ltd, Glasgow

ISBN 0 00 675390 6

for Louise

Prologue

Long ago and far away, on the great snow-covered steppe of Russia, a small boy and a wolfcub found themselves lost in the snow, sheltering in the same small wooden hut. Now, as everyone knows, wolves and people should be frightened of each other, but not these two. Each was cold and alone and a long way from home. They decided that the only way to survive was to make friends.

The boy, Sasha, was found by his father and taken back to his village. The wolfcub, Ferdy, eventually found his own way back to his pack. People and wolves were still frightened of each other, but Sasha and Ferdy remained friends... even after they grew up.

Then one day, Ivan, Sasha's father, the village elder and a great wolfhater, was buried under a snowdrift. Because of his friendship with Sasha, Ferdy dug Ivan out and saved his life. After that the villagers began to realise that not all wolves were wicked, and the wolves in Ferdy's pack and the people in Sasha's village became firm friends. In the winter, when food was short, the villagers put out food for the wolves, and in better times they all danced happily together.

Chapter One

Sasha pulled his hat down over his ears against the cold wind. He straightened up, stretched his back and looked out over the great Russian steppe. As he did so, he noticed the last tiny brown leaf fall from a tree… Winter was nearly here and the snow would soon be too deep to wander far from the village. Sasha flung his huge bundle of sticks up on to his back and started to trudge home with the weight bearing down on him. He looked down into the valley and saw his village; the painted wooden houses, the church with the onion domes, the great house and the duck pond. Smoke was spiralling out of the chimneys of the houses – how cosy and welcoming they looked.

As Sasha trudged along, he noticed something new – teams of horses dragging great logs from the forests down to the valley. "Hmmm," thought Sasha. "They must be for the great railroad that Father told me about. My goodness, what a difference that will make to our lives! Who knows, maybe I will even get to leave the village and explore the great wide world."

Suddenly, Sasha heard a crunching of branches. Then a familiar voice called out,

"Psst! Psst, Sasha man-child, come here a minute! I want to ask you something."

Sasha grinned broadly. "Ferdy," he cried, "what a lovely surprise!" And he climbed up the bank towards the wolf.

"Ferdy, my old friend, how are you?" he asked, shaking the wolf enthusiastically by the paw.

"I am perfectly all right, of course I am," snapped the wolf. "Wolves are always all right."

"Oh," said Sasha. "Well, that's good, but then why are you so keen to talk to me?"

"Because I want you to tell me what's going on."

"Nothing's going on. I don't know what you're talking about."

"'Course you do," said the wolf crossly.

"'Course you know what's going on. And if you deny it I'll bite your nose and…"

"Yes, I know, and eat my toes. I'm sorry, Ferdy, but I really don't know what you mean."

"Down there," replied the wolf, "down in the valley, those men. What are they doing?"

"Oh," cried Sasha, "silly me, you mean the railway! Those men are putting down tracks for the trains to move along."

"Railway, tracks, trains? Never heard of them," sniffed the wolf. "Now you tell me what they're for, man-child, or I'll…"

"Bite my ears and eat my toes," repeated Sasha.

"No, not at all, nothing so merciful. I will gobble you up in one big bite."

"No, you won't," said Sasha, laughing, "because I am your very old friend, and if you eat me up, you'll never learn what the railways are all about."

"That is true," said Ferdy, grinning. "That is perfectly true."

"Well, I don't know much about

railways," said Sasha. "I've never even seen one. But Father has. When he went to the market in Ponsk he saw one, and he hasn't stopped talking about it since. So come on, come home with me. Mother and Father will be delighted to see you, and Father will tell you all about railways. And I mean *all*."

"Hmmm," grumbled the wolf. "Do you know what's for supper? Then I'll decide."

"I'm not sure," Sasha told him, "but when I left this morning Mother was scrubbing beets and chopping onions."

"Borscht!" yelled the wolf, "my favourite! I'll race you to the house. Last one there's a hairy kipper!"

"That's not fair!" shouted Sasha, "I've got the heavy bundle to carry."

"Tough luck, man-child," called the wolf.

He raced off through the woods, which were lightly covered in snow that gleamed pink in the sunset. Sasha struggled after him, but it was dark before he reached the village. The lights shining in the windows of the wooden houses were warm and welcoming. When Sasha arrived at the door, panting and holding his side, Ferdy was already seated at the table with a napkin tied round his neck and holding his spoon up in readiness.

"Hello, hairy kipper," he said, grinning, while Sasha's mother Olga piled the rich, red, steaming soup into his bowl. "Hurry up and sit down. I can't wait to get going on this delicious soup." And he sniffed appreciatively.

"That wolf!" roared Ivan. "He doesn't change. Sasha, sit down, it's your favourite meal too."

So they sat round the table and ate the soup, with sour cream and potatoes floating in it and delicious bits of green spring onion on the top.

After eating three helpings, Ferdy blew a kiss to Olga. "This soup is divine," he said. "I dream of it when I am running on the wild cold steppe, and when I actually eat it, it is even better than my dreams." And he wiped his mouth with his napkin and smiled at them all.

"Ferdy has something to ask you, Father," said Sasha.

"Ask away my friend," smiled Ivan. "What can I do for you?"

"Well," said Ferdy, "Sasha man-child says that all those men doing odd things down in the valley are building a rail whatsit."

"A railway, yes. Isn't it exciting? Soon we will have trains going through our little village, and life will never be quite the same again."

"Explain it to me, please," demanded the wolf.

"A train is a miracle, Ferdy. You never saw anything so amazing in your life. In front there is an engine driven by steam which makes a noise like this." And Ivan made the sound of a steam engine starting up.

"Ha!" laughed Ferdy, "you're having me on. Now really, what is a rail whatsit?"

"I'm telling you the truth, Ferdy! And behind the engine is a series of large boxes with seats in them where people can sit. Then it moves very fast like this." And Ivan went round the room making the sound of a train going along, "chuffety chuff, chuffety chuff."

Ferdy laughed. "Your dad has lost his

marbles, Sasha! But it's a good story."

"It's no story!" yelled Ivan.

"Then what have those bits of metal out there got to do with this chuffety chuff thing?"

"Those are rail tracks," Ivan explained. "The train moves on wheels, but they need the tracks to slide on. That's what they are doing out there, laying the tracks for the train to go on. The train stops at a station and picks up passengers. Then – chuffety chuff! The train takes the passengers to where they want to go, in no time and for very little money. Like I said, I saw it with my own eyes when I went to Ponsk."

"Does that mean that we will be able to travel to places far away, Father?" asked Sasha, his eyes shining with excitement.

"Yes, Sasha my boy. We can all go to Ponsk together."

"I'll be able to see my Auntie Marya!" cried Olga, "and eat ice cream!"

"And I'll be able to go and buy the best seed in the market," added Ivan, "and grow better crops."

"And I could go to the college there!" said Sasha excitedly.

"Could wolves go on the rail whatsit?" demanded Ferdy.

"No!" cried Ivan, Sasha and Olga, all at once.

"Just for people then?" moaned the wolf.

"Yes," agreed Ivan. "But just think of it! Within weeks we will be able to see the trains as they go past our own village. How much bigger our world will become. Oh Ferdy, what times are coming!"

"This train on the metal tracks, does it go fast?" enquired Ferdy.

"Very fast."

"Faster than horses?"

"Oh, much faster than horses."

"Hmmm," said the wolf, a sad look coming into his eyes. "So lots of new people will be able to come to our village."

"Yes," agreed Ivan. "Is that so terrible?"

"Yes, very terrible," moaned Ferdy. "None of the new people will realise how nice we wolves are. They will be afraid of us and want to shoot us. Something tells me that this rail whatsit will be very bad news for wolves. Very bad news indeed."

Chapter Two

Spring came, and the silver tracks of the railway began to push out beyond the village and into the vastness of the great steppe. Sasha and Ferdy stood on a rock above the village and looked at the silver snake of the railway going further and further and further.

"What now, Sasha man-child?" asked the wolf in a worried tone.

"I'm not sure," Sasha replied. "I suppose a station will be built and then the trains will start to run."

"Station?" grumbled Ferdy. "What's a station, when it's at home?"

"I've never seen one," Sasha told him, "but I've seen pictures."

"I don't care whether you've actually seen one or not," snapped Ferdy, "what I want to know is what a station is *like*. Now, are you going to tell me or are you not?"

"Keep your hair on, Ferdy," laughed Sasha.

"Not *hair*, dear boy, *fur*, if you don't mind," the wolf retorted.

Sasha laughed and rubbed Ferdy's head.

"Why are you so short-tempered these days, Ferdy?" he asked.

"It's all this change, Sasha man-child," sighed Ferdy. "I don't like it, and I'm trying to work out what is happening, and you don't give me the information I need."

"I'm not holding out on you, Ferdy, I just don't know much about railways myself. But I'll try and describe a station."

"Here, take this stick and draw it in the dust," Ferdy instructed him.

So Sasha drew a picture of the platforms where the train stopped and the room where the tickets were sold and the waiting room and the area outside where the carriages could pick people up.

"How does it work, this station thing?"

"Well," said Sasha slowly, "what I think happens is that the train comes into the station, chuffety chuff…"

"Chuffety chuff?" questioned Ferdy.

"Well, er, yes. Well, that's what Father said, the wheels go round and make that noise. Chuffety chuff. Then the train stops and people open doors and get off at the station."

"Yes."

"And then more people get on, and off it goes again."

"Chuffety chuff," said Ferdy.

"Exactly," agreed Sasha.

"Mmmm," said Ferdy, shaking his head, "it's all very hard to imagine, Sasha man-child. But in a few months I expect the station thing will be finished."

"Probably," nodded Sasha.

"Will there be a big celebration?" asked the wolf.

"Oh yes, I heard Father talking about it. The man who owns the railway is coming to take part in the ceremony, and all the village bands for miles around are coming to play."

"Good," said Ferdy, grinning. "You know how much we wolves love music. Oh well, maybe the rail whatsit and the station thing are not such a bad idea after all. Will there be lots of food?"

"Oh course," smiled Sasha, "and loads to drink."

"And dancing?" asked Ferdy hopefully.

"And dancing," nodded Sasha.

They both laughed and began to dance together, leaping as high as they could.

When the day for the opening of the station was announced, Ivan and Sasha went to find Ferdy to tell the wolves about the celebration.

"We'll be there, don't you worry. We'll be there," Ferdy assured them. "And I hope there's going to be plenty of meat dumplings, because they're my favourite."

The opening of the station was the biggest event Sasha could ever remember. The band from the local town was there, all dressed in red coats with gold braid. The Mayor of the town had come too, and the owner of the railway company, and people from all over the area. After a while the music stopped, and the owner of the railway company began a speech.

"Ladies and gentlemen of Pogibursk, it is with great pleasure that I declare this station open."

He was just about to cut the ribbon when someone screamed "Wolves! Wolves! Lots of them!"

Ferdy and his pack were walking down the street towards the station.

"Wolves! Run for it!" shrieked someone, and everyone scattered.

"It's all right," shouted Sasha, "they are our wolves, they're friends! They won't hurt you."

"That's right," cried Ivan. "I assure you they've only come here to dance."

But no one listened. A moment later, a shot rang out.

Ferdy looked surprised. "What's happening, Sasha man-child? We only came to dance."

"Run!" yelled Ivan, "run away! They don't understand about wolves. Run, Ferdy! Run for your lives, wolves!"

So the wolves turned tail and raced out of the village so fast that none of the bullets touched them.

"Oh Father," groaned Sasha, "what are we going to do? All our hard work making wolves and people friends, undone in five minutes!"

"Sasha my boy, don't despair," said Ivan, slapping Sasha on the shoulder. "We were stupid not to expect this. Think how long it took me to come round to the idea that people can be friends with wolves. We'll have to educate these people – it will take time. Now off you go and find Ferdy and explain to him that the strangers were just a bit scared."

So Sasha went walking in the woods, calling out: "Ferdy! Ferdy, where are you? It's me, Sasha! I need to talk to you!"

Sasha heard a rustling in the undergrowth, and there stood Ferdy.

"Why didn't you warn us that there would be men with guns?" he demanded. "Huh, some friend you are."

"Sorry, Ferdy," said Sasha, "we just didn't think. Father says we should have realised that most people are still scared of wolves. He says you must stay out of the way until the strangers have gone."

"People," sniffed Ferdy disapprovingly. "Honestly, what a bunch of ninnies."

"They're not ninnies, Ferdy," Sasha told him, "but they've been brought up to be scared of wolves. Father says they only need a bit of time and education."

"I told you this rail whatsit would be bad for wolves," Ferdy informed him. "And so far, it has been. In my opinion, the strangers will need a lot of time and huge amounts of education. Until then, there won't be much dancing for us wolves."

Chapter Three

Soon after the railway station was opened, a huge sawmill was built close to the railway line. All day, trees went into the mill and came out as logs. Then they were taken by train to the big cities. New people were brought in from a nearby town to work at the sawmill, and a little settlement of millworkers grew up by the station.

Sasha was sitting looking at the sawmill

thoughtfully one day, when someone tickled his neck. He turned, and there was Ferdy brushing his tail across Sasha's neck.

"Hello, Ferdy," he said enthusiastically. "Good to see you, old friend."

"Less of the old," grumbled Ferdy. "What's going on here? One of the pack told me there was a new building, so I came to check it out."

"It's a sawmill," Sasha told him.

"I hope you know what that is," snapped the wolf, "or I'll bite your ears…"

"And eat my toes, I know," laughed Sasha.

"Well actually, you don't know," continued Ferdy, "because what I *was* going to say was 'lick your nose'." And he gave Sasha a big wet lick.

"Ferdy, stop it!" yelled Sasha as he rolled over laughing and Ferdy jumped on top of him.

Suddenly they heard a shot and shouts of "Wolves! Wolves! Hide! Danger!"

Ferdy leapt up and began to snarl.

"It's the new people from the sawmill," Sasha said quickly. "Run, Ferdy, they don't understand! Run for it! I'll talk to you later."

Ferdy bounded off into the woods as Sasha got to his feet.

"Are you all right?" asked one man. "Good thing we were so close and heard that wolf or you'd be dead by now."

"That wolf was my friend Ferdy," Sasha told them indignantly. "I wasn't in the least danger, and you just broke up a very pleasant conversation."

The crowd round Sasha looked amazed for a moment. Then they began to laugh.

"He's joking! It's all right, he's just joking. He's not mad, just having a laugh at our expense."

"Yeah, I've heard his father talk the same way," complained someone. "Just because we're new to this village, it doesn't mean we're daft, you know. A wolf is a wolf and no friend to man."

"You don't know what you're talking about!" yelled Sasha. "In this village we made friends with the wolves and they don't kill our animals any more. It's wonderful and I'm not letting you spoil it!" And he strode off towards his home feeling very angry.

That night, Ivan called a meeting of all the villagers at his home.

"It's to discuss the problem of the new people and the wolves," Sasha told everyone.

"Don't worry, we'll be there," everyone promised.

Later, Ivan's house was packed to overflowing. Ivan looked around. "Thank you for coming at such short notice, everyone. The only person who's missing is Sasha."

"I saw him walking into the woods, Ivan," said Old Peter.

"Why would my son go walking in the woods at night?" frowned Ivan.

"To find me!" came a familiar voice, and Ferdy jumped in through the window. Sasha followed through the door, smiling.

"Ferdy!" cried everyone, and they crowded round the wolf, hugging him and shaking his paw. "It's great to see you! We are all so upset about what has been happening."

"Make sure that our special guest has a

big plate of food," called Ivan, "and then the meeting must start."

So Ferdy was given a plate piled high with all his favourite things.

"I made your favourite dumplings," cried Lushka, "just in case you came."

"And I cooked my delicious liver pie," added Old Peter.

"And we kept a whole loaf of my white bread with poppy seeds," smiled Grushka.

Ferdy grinned at all his friends. "You really restore my faith in people," he told them, and began to tuck into the food with relish.

When every last crumb had gone, Ferdy looked fondly at the sea of human faces around him.

"Dear friends," he said, "what a sad turn of events. Just when we had everything so pleasantly sorted."

"Absolutely!" agreed Sasha.

"No doubt about it," shouted Ivan, and

he banged his fist on the table.

"Definitely," nodded Olga.

"Hear, hear," cried everyone else.

"But what are we going to do about it?" demanded Sasha.

There was a long silence.

"No one got any ideas?" asked Ferdy. "Not even one very little idea?"

"Well, I've got an idea," said Lushka. "There's a big cave down by the river just off the Beluga road. I used to go there when I was courting Anatoly. No one ever goes there."

"I know that cave," nodded Ferdy, "but what about it?"

"We could take food there and stock it up for winter, so that you wolves can go and get something if you feel hungry."

"And not come near the village, you mean?"

Lushka nodded sadly. "I wish it wasn't necessary, Ferdy, but yes, you wolves keep away from the village until we manage to talk our new neighbours round."

"Why don't I just talk to them?" suggested Ferdy. "That would be the sensible thing to do. Explain to them how wonderful I am and all that."

"No!" cried Sasha and Ivan and Olga together.

"It's too risky," agreed everyone. "Please don't even think of it, Ferdy."

"Yes, dear friend, we must give them time," declared Ivan, putting his arm round Ferdy. "Time is what they need, and time is what they must have."

"But don't worry," the crowd assured him, "you won't go hungry, we'll see to that."

Chapter Four

As the next winter approached and the first light snowfalls began, the villagers started to stock up the cave for Ferdy and his pack. Most days, Ferdy stood at the entrance and told people where to put what.

"The liver pies right inside where it's coldest. The soups over here please, and the meat in front of the pies."

When it was all done, the wolves and the

villagers looked at the packed cave with satisfaction.

"Even if it's a particularly long winter we'll not go hungry," said Ferdy, grinning, "so you people will be safe for one more year."

"I wish you could come into the village and fetch the food like in the old days," grumbled Old Peter. "It was a bit of company for me, and you wolves are always so appreciative of my cooking."

Everyone else murmured agreement.

"Well," said Ferdy cheerfully, "then it's up to you lot to get the other lot to see sense. That's your task for the winter." And he ran off into the falling snow, laughing, with the rest of the pack on his heels.

But when the villagers got back to the

village, they found they hardly had anything to do with the new settlers at the sawmill. The newcomers thought the villagers were a bit mad because of their attitude to the wolves, and the villagers were angry about Ferdy, so there was no mixing. Then one day, something happened to change all of that.

Because they knew that the long cold winter was setting in, everyone went into the woods to get big stocks of firewood for the freezing nights. While the newcomers collected wood on one side of the river bank, the villagers were busily chopping logs on the other side.

Olga looked up as she put a log in her basket, and saw a woman put her baby down in a bed of leaves near the river.

"She shouldn't do that," Olga told Sasha. "The river sometimes has flash floods, it's dangerous."

"Hey!" Sasha called over the water. "My mother thinks you should move your baby away from the river for safety."

"My baby's well enough!" snapped the woman, and went on collecting sticks.

Sasha shrugged his shoulders and continued cutting logs, but Olga looked worried. "I wish she'd listen," she sighed. "They're new to the village, they don't understand about the river."

The next day, Sasha, Ivan and Olga were busy collecting firewood for the long winter again, like everyone else.

"Look," Olga muttered to her son. "Just

look, that woman's left her baby by the river again. Do you think I should say something?"

"You'll just get snapped at, Mother, like I got snapped at yesterday. Better leave it."

"No, I can't do that," said Olga shaking her head. "Excuse me my dear!" she called. "May I suggest you move your baby to higher ground?"

"I told you yesterday," snapped the woman, "my baby's fine, just fine."

Just then Ivan came riding down to the river, shouting at the top of his voice: "Move, move to higher ground, everyone! The dam upstream is bursting at its seams! Come on, grab your sticks and move, better safe than sorry!"

The villagers grabbed their bundles and

scrambled up their side of the river bank. Some of the sawmill workers went to follow.

"Ignore him!" cried their leader. "It's a trick! They just want us out of here, so that they can have all the wood for themselves and their friends the wolves."

The workers roared with laughter.

"You crazy people!" bellowed Ivan, his eyes flashing. "You don't know this river like we do. For pity's sake, do as I say!"

Suddenly there was a rush of water. They all turned to look at the river. The angry water was rising fast.

Then a horrible cry echoed across the valley.

"My baby! Oh no! She's not here, she's been carried away by the river!"

Everyone on both sides of the bank

stopped what they were doing and froze with horror. Ivan instantly took charge.

"Sasha, you take a party down river, on this side. All the old villagers go with Sasha!"

Then Ivan plunged into the swelling water on his horse and beckoned to the newcomers crying: "Come with me, we'll go along this bank! The river has flooded but it still isn't moving very fast. With a bit of luck we may still find the baby."

Everyone did as Ivan told them, and the weeping mother was led away by her husband.

When night fell, the baby still hadn't been found. Torches were lit and the search went on well into the night. An icy wind blew across the steppe. The wind whistled in the freezing night air and the branches of the trees waved around angrily. Outside the village the howl of the wolves could be heard. Finally the searchers gave up. There was not even the smallest sign of the baby. A very sad crowd gathered outside Ivan's house as the snow began to fall fast and thick.

"Did anyone find any clues?" asked Ivan hopefully. "A bit of blanket or anything?"

The crowd shook their heads miserably.

A man came out from the crowd and stood next to Ivan on the porch. "Friends, my name is Grisha," he said quietly. "I want to thank you all on behalf of my wife

Ludmilla and myself, for your help in the search for our daughter Minka. I only wish our efforts had been successful, and that we had been sensible and listened to people with more experience." And he wiped away a tear.

Ivan put his arms round the man and gave him a hug. Soon the old villagers and the newcomers were all comforting each other.

"Pity it took something like this to bring us together," sighed Ivan. "A great pity."

The winter turned out to be a long and hard one, and the village was cut off on all sides by huge falls of rock and snow. For months, no one could get in or out of the village, even by train.

"Do you think Ferdy and the pack will be all right?" Sasha asked his parents over supper one night.

"Of course they'll be all right!" roared Ivan. "Wolves love the snow, and they won't have gone hungry."

"It's a comfort to know that," agreed Olga, "but I do miss the wolves, particularly Ferdy."

"Me too," nodded Sasha.

"Maybe next winter will be different," commented Ivan. "I mean, the whole atmosphere in the village has improved. The newcomers don't seem so new any more and we all get on now. I think they'll listen to us when we explain about the wolves."

"I hope so," said Sasha with a sigh, "I

really do hope so."

When the snow began to melt at last, Ivan went and got his sleigh.

"Sasha, get the horses!" he cried. "Let's take a ride out on to the great white steppe and see if we can find any wolves."

"Great idea, Father," laughed Sasha. "Let's see if we can get as far as the cave. Ferdy will probably be there."

"I think so too. Ferdy will be so upset to hear the news about the baby. Come on Sasha, in you get. Let's go!"

And off they went over the snow, travelling as fast as the wind towards Ferdy's cave.

Chapter Five

Ivan and Ferdy laughed as the horse-drawn sleigh raced across the wide white steppe.

"It feels great to be out of the village at last, Father!" Sasha cried.

"The end of winter is always a happy time," agreed his father. "Soon we'll have our spring celebration and lots of dancing."

"I hope dear old Ferdy will be able to come and join in as usual," sighed Sasha.

Just then they came within sight of the cave. Warned by the sound of the sleigh bells, Ferdy came running out.

"Welcome!" he cried, "welcome man-child, welcome Ivan!"

"So Ferdy, have you had a good winter?" asked Ivan, giving the wolf a hug.

"Very good," smiled Ferdy.

"Did the stocks of food last out?" demanded Sasha.

"They most certainly did. And it's just as well, because the most wonderful thing happened. We had an extra mouth to feed."

"Another cub?" asked Sasha.

"No, not a cub, silly. A baby."

"A baby!" cried Sasha and Ivan together.

"Yes," Ferdy told them excitedly, "a real

live human baby. Some nasty mother threw the baby away, and it got carried away by the river. It was sailing downstream, when my good wife saw it and pulled it out of the river. My goodness! What a good thing she was there, or that poor baby would be very dead."

"What did you do with the baby?" asked Sasha, hardly daring to breathe.

"What do you mean, what did I do with it? Fed it of course, kept it warm, played with it. What else would a wolf do with a baby? Come and look, my she-wolf is the best mother in the world."

Ivan and Sasha followed Ferdy into the cave, and there playing happily on the cave floor was a baby, laughing with joy.

Sasha and Ivan looked with amazement at the naked baby as it happily rolled around on the floor, fighting with Ferdy's cubs and giving wolf-like shrieks of pleasure.

"Sasha, go and find the mother quickly, there's not a moment to waste!" cried Ivan.

"Why bother telling her?" sniffed Ferdy. "She doesn't care. She didn't take any care of her baby, she threw it away, just threw it away, I told you. I saw her with my own eyes!"

"No, my friend," said Ivan, "she certainly didn't throw the baby away."

"Then why did she put it down in the leaves on the river bank? Answer me that."

"Because she was new to the area and she didn't realise that the river would flood."

"Huh!" Ferdy snorted. "Didn't realise that the river would flood, didn't realise that wolves were wonderful. What's the matter with the woman? People! Honestly, I do not know, I really do not."

"You'd better go and explain to your wife what happened, Ferdy," Sasha told the wolf in a low voice. "The baby is going to have to go back to its mother."

"Baby's much better off with a wolf for a mother," grumbled Ferdy.

"You've got to do it, Ferdy," said Sasha sternly. "You've got to explain it."

"Oh all right," moaned the wolf, and he went over to his mate.

"Dearest," he began, taking her paw. "My lovely Nina, it seems the person-mother didn't throw the baby away after all, it was an accident. Would you believe it, she didn't know the river might flood. So, er, well, we'll have to give the baby back to her because she has been so very sad."

A tear ran down the she-wolf's nose. Ferdy picked up the baby gently.

"I'm glad this baby's going back," he muttered. "Silly things, human babies.

They've got no teeth, they've got no fur, they've got no claws. Useless if you ask me. I mean, how could a baby survive on the great white steppe? We're better off without it."

And Ferdy handed the baby over to Sasha, who covered it in kisses and then wrapped it in a big fur blanket.

Ivan and Sasha drove back to the village as fast as they could. Sasha looked back and saw that the cubs were all running after the sleigh, barking and howling.

"Why are those silly wolves following us?" demanded Ivan.

"I think they see the baby as one of the pack and as their sister," answered Sasha. "They don't want to lose her."

"Well Sasha, we have to return the baby to her mother. There isn't any choice. The cubs will just have to get used to it."

"Of course, Father," agreed Sasha.

"But I do hope Ludmilla will understand about our wolves, once she's got her baby back."

Chapter Six

The sleigh carrying Ivan and Sasha and the baby Minka swept into the village, with the wolfcubs running behind barking. Then Sasha looked up and saw a gun pointing at the wolfcubs from one of the upstairs windows.

"No!" he shouted, holding up the baby. "No, don't shoot! We've got the baby! The wolves looked after her all winter, she's a fine bonny girl, look!"

To Sasha's relief the gun disappeared and a cry went through the village.

"The baby's been found! She's safe and well, the wolves looked after her, go and tell Ludmilla that her baby's all right. God be praised!"

The baby's mother ran out of her house towards the sleigh, her arms outstretched. Ivan reined in the horses and Sasha handed her the baby.

"Oh thank you, thank you!" she cried, "a thousand, thousand thanks!"

"Don't thank us!" bellowed Ivan. "Thank the wolves. They rescued her from drowning and looked after her all winter."

Ludmilla looked at the wolfcubs leaping

up and barking at her baby, and then at Ferdy and his wife, who had followed their cubs into the town. Then Ludmilla burst into tears, and went and hugged Ferdy and his wife.

"What can I ever do to repay you?" she asked.

"You could let our little ones visit their sister," Ferdy told her. "They think your baby is their sister."

"Of course they can visit her," Ludmilla told them, and put the baby down on the ground. The wolfcubs jumped on her and licked her as she giggled with delight.

Just then, Grisha the baby's father arrived on the scene. "My daughter, where is she?" he demanded.

The crowd separated for him, and there

lay his daughter laughing contentedly. Grisha gathered up his daughter and kissed her all over.

"You wolves need never worry about food again," he told Ferdy. "From now on, every winter I will feed you, even if it means going hungry myself."

"Thanks a bundle," said Ferdy, "but we get fed anyway. All we wolves want from you is to be able to come and go, and dance at your festivals."

"Dance?!"

"Yes, dance. It is a good thing that people dance. I am the champion dancer in the neighbourhood, and I want to be able to come and join in the dancing and the jumping."

"It's a deal," cried Grisha. "But no one

can jump higher than me, friend wolf. I challenge you to a jumping competition."

Ferdy caught Sasha's eye and grinned.

"I accept your challenge, friend man, with pleasure," he said.

"Good!" shouted Ivan, "we will all look forward to that! And as the head man of the village, I invite you wolves to be our guests of honour at our celebration for the end of winter next Saturday."

"Saturday it is," agreed Ferdy, "and my family and myself and the rest of the pack would be delighted to be the guests of honour. Glad to see that you have learned how to treat wolves at last. See you next Saturday." Then he barked sharply at the cubs, who reluctantly fell into line and followed their parents back to the cave.

The following Saturday was the biggest feast the village had ever had. Everyone ate and ate. Ferdy sat in between Sasha and Ludmilla, who kept planting sloppy wet kisses on his head.

"Make her stop it," Ferdy whispered fiercely to Sasha, "or I'll bite her nose and eat her ears and…"

"I get the picture," Sasha replied, laughing. He stood up and banged on the table. "Ferdy wants the jumping competition to begin," he declared. "Band, get to your places! Then we can see who jumps the best."

So the band scuttled to get their instruments and climbed on to the platform. It was the biggest band the village had ever had, because five of the newcomers played instruments. The music struck up. Grisha leapt up and went and stood by Ferdy, who was pulling on his shiny leather boots. As the band played a rousing tune, the two of them leapt, higher and higher. In the end, however, Grisha had to admit that Ferdy could leap higher than him.

"No man ever managed to jump higher than me," Grisha told Ferdy.

"No, well, they wouldn't," replied Ferdy casually, "but wolves are good, very, *very* good, at jumping."

Ivan climbed on to the platform and signalled to the band to stop playing.

"Friends," he cried, "I can't tell you how happy it makes me to see all you people and wolves having so much fun together. For a while, we were two communities in a small place, and that was all wrong. But now we are united, and that is so good. Now, our new friends from the sawmill came to see me yesterday and said that they wanted to do something special for the wolves to make up for their untrusting and suspicious behaviour. So Ferdy, before I formally present you with the champion's cup once again, is there anything you or your pack would like?"

Ferdy joined Ivan on the platform.

"Yes," he declared, "there is something we want. A ride on the rail whatsit."

There was a deathly silence.

"Wolves can't go on a train," said Ivan in confusion after a minute.

"Why not?" demanded Ferdy angrily. "You just explain to me why not."

"Well, they can't, that's all. For one thing, all the people on the train would be terrified."

"People," grumbled Ferdy. "All anyone ever thinks about is people. Typical. Ask you what you want, and when you tell them, they say, 'Oh, it's not possible, Ferdy. Think of something else, Ferdy. Don't be so unrealistic, Ferdy.' Don't know why you even bother to ask. Come on Nina, come on cubs, come on pack, we're going back to our cave."

"No!" shouted Sasha. "No, Ferdy! Listen, I've got an idea. Why don't we all take a train ride to Trellin, down the line, and pretend that the wolves are our dogs?"

A murmur went up.

"I'd love a train ride! Yes, we could pretend the wolves were our dogs. What a good idea! Well done, Sasha!"

"Will that be all right, Ferdy?" asked Sasha.

"No, it certainly won't be all right,"

sniffed the wolf. "Wolves can't pretend to be dogs! We are creatures of the wild, free as the wind. Dogs are silly wolves who have been tamed and have learned to serve man. Wolves gone soft, that's what they are."

"Well then, no train ride, Ferdy," said Sasha sadly, shaking his head. "I just cannot think of another way of getting you and the rest of the pack on to a train."

"Well, if it's the only way, we'll do it," grumbled Ferdy, looking very cross.

So the very next Saturday, the whole village was lined up in their best clothes on the brand-new railway station. The wolves were there too, all brushed and wearing very grand red collars with studs and leads that gleamed in the spring sunlight. People from other villages who were standing on the station looked on with curiosity at the large party of dogs. Among them was a young woman with a long blonde plait. Ferdy stared at her very hard, then he jumped up to Sasha and whispered in his ear:

"That girl with the long plait, what do you think of her?"

"She looks very nice," replied Sasha, pretending to stroke Ferdy's head as if he were a dog.

"Go and talk to her then," growled Ferdy. "High time you had a wife."

"I can't just go up and talk to her," whispered Sasha. "I mean, she might not like me, and I'm too scared."

"Sasha man-child, I'm ashamed of you,"
sniffed Ferdy, and he ran over to the girl.
Then he grabbed her skirt in his teeth and
growled and tore off a piece of material.

"Grrr," said Ferdy cheerfully. "Grrrrrrr! Woof, woof!"

Sasha raced over, grabbed Ferdy by his brand-new red collar and dragged him back.

"I am so sorry," cried Sasha, "I don't know what got into Fer—, my dog. He doesn't usually behave like that. Oh dear, and your pretty skirt is all torn! Please let me buy you another one."

"It doesn't matter, really it doesn't," said the girl, smiling at Sasha.

"It does, of course it does," insisted Sasha. "I'll get something done about it, really I will. Ferdy doesn't usually behave like that. Please, what's your name?"

"Tatyana," the girl told him.

Ferdy gave a little howl of triumph. At

that moment Olga came hurrying up.

"I've just heard about what Ferdy did, how terrible! My dear, I am Sasha's mother and an excellent needlewoman. Please let me make you another skirt. I absolutely insist."

"Well, all right," smiled Tatyana. "That would be wonderful."

"We live in the big house there, just behind the station," Olga told her. "Come over tomorrow."

"I shall look forward to it," agreed Tatyana.

"There you go," sniffed Ferdy under his breath. "Piece of cake. Easy as falling off a log. Leave it to a wolf, that's what I always say."

Just then, the train puffed into the

station. Everyone cheered and excitedly clambered into the train carriages. Ferdy, Nina and the cubs climbed up and put their paws on the window ledge. They all looked out, barking with delight.

As the train puffed its way across the vast steppe and raced past woods and forests, tiny villages and small towns, crossing fast rivers on high bridges and chugging through tunnels, everyone had a wonderful time. The villagers got out their picnics and passed food around. Ferdy and the wolves ate as much as they could, and enjoyed being stroked and fussed over while they watched the world whizz past.

"Ha!" Ferdy told Sasha. "This rail whatsit is great!"

"You didn't always think that," Sasha reminded him.

"I know," grinned Ferdy, "but I'm glad I was wrong, very glad indeed. Just look at us racing across the countryside even faster than the wind, faster than anything! This is the life. *Oorá!*"

It will not surprise you to learn that everyone who worked at the sawmill learned to love Ferdy and his family just as much as Sasha and the other villagers did. Sasha and Tatyana got married just as Ferdy had planned, and during the long hard winters, the wolves got food from everyone.

"More than we can eat sometimes," Ferdy whispered to Sasha.

And whenever there was a festivity, the wolves came down into the village as before, and the sound of wolves and people enjoying themselves together rang across the great Russian steppe.

SASHA AND THE WOLFCUB
by Ann Jungman

"You're not very big for a wolf," said Sasha.
"And you're not very big for a man,"
snapped the wolf.

Sasha is always being warned about wolves –
they're cruel and dangerous, especially when
hungry. But then he gets lost in the snow... and a
little wolfcub roams too far from his pack. Both
must forget the warnings if they are to survive a
snowy Russian winter...

Another Collins Red Storybook
to add to your collection!

Collins
An Imprint of HarperCollinsPublishers
www.fireandwater.com

THE WITCH'S TEARS
by Jenny Nimmo

In freezing hail and howling wind, a stranger is given shelter at Theo's house – a stranger who loves telling stories and whose name is Mrs Scarum. Theo is convinced she's a witch and wishes his father would return home from his travels. But the blizzard continues and the night is long... and there may be tears before morning.

Another Collins Red Storybook to add to your collection!

Collins

An Imprint of HarperCollins*Publishers*

www.fireandwater.com

MAX, THE BOY WHO MADE A MILLION

by Gyles Brandreth

*"You're going to have to be brave, boy —
brave and strong."*

When Max's father is arrested for something he
didn't do, Max runs away and joins up with the
Great Zapristi — Master of Illusion — Famous the
World Over! Max *must* clear his father's name
and earn enough money to get him out of prison.
Dare he do it as Maximilian Rich, the Boy Who
Walks the Tightrope? Max's riproaring
adventures take him from the streets of 1890s
New York to the Niagara Falls — through lions'
cages, storms at sea and dazzling feats of bravery.

*Another Collins Red Storybook
to add to your collection!*

Collins

An Imprint of HarperCollinsPublishers
www.fireandwater.com

THE PUPPY PRESENT
by Jean Ure

Just one small puppy in need of some people…

Ginger and James are two of a kind, even though Ginger is a puppy and James is a boy. Both want to be loved and cared for. But Ginger's young owner gets fed up with her puppy, and James's parents get fed up with his tantrums. Ginger and James must take drastic action to find their own future happiness.

Another Collins Red Storybook to add to your collection!

Collins
An Imprint of HarperCollinsPublishers
www.fireandwater.com

HAPPY BIRTHDAY, SPIDER MCDREW
by Alan Durant and Martin Chatterton

Spider McDrew is a hopeless case. Everybody says so. He is always saying and doing the wrong thing. He gets the punchlines to his jokes wrong; he daydreams in class; he always has odd socks on; and he even gets into a muddle over his own birthday party invitations. Spider McDrew is a hopeless case who's great just the way he is!

Three more lively stories about Spider McDrew – the hopeless case who can't help becoming a hero!

*Another Collins Red Storybook
to add to your collection!*

Collins

An Imprint of HarperCollinsPublishers
www.fireandwater.com

Order Form

To order direct from the publishers, just make a list of the titles you want and fill in the form below:

Name ....

Address ....

....

....

Send to: Dept 6, HarperCollins Publishers Ltd, Westerhill Road, Bishopbriggs, Glasgow G64 2QT.

Please enclose a cheque or postal order to the value of the cover price, plus:

UK & BFPO: Add £1.00 for the first book, and 25p per copy for each additional book ordered.

Overseas and Eire: Add £2.95 service charge. Books will be sent by surface mail but quotes for airmail despatch will be given on request.

A 24-hour telephone ordering service is available to holders of Visa, MasterCard, Amex or Switch cards on 0141- 772 2281.

Collins
An *Imprint of* HarperCollins*Publishers*